I Can Make

HOLIDAY GIFTS

Makerspace
Projects

Emily Reid

WINDMILL
BOOKS ™

New York

Published in 2016 by **Windmill Books**, an Imprint of Rosen Publishing
29 East 21st Street, New York, NY 10010

Developed and produced for Rosen by BlueAppleWorks Inc.

Creative Director: Melissa McClellan
Managing Editor for BlueAppleWorks: Melissa McClellan
Designer: T.J. Choleva
Photo Research: Jane Reid
Editor: Marcia Abramson
Craft Artisans: Jerrie McClellan (p. 8, 10, 12, 16, 18, 20, 24, 30); Sarah Hodgson (p. 14, 22, 26, 28)

Photo Credits: cover center image Blend Images/Bigstock; title page, TOC, p. 5 second row right, p. 6
bottom, 8–9, 10–11, 12–13, 14–15, 16–17, 18–19, 20–21, 22–23, 24–25, 26–27, 28-29, 30 Austen Photography;
p. 4 left, 5 first row Photka/Dreamstime; p. 4 right Ermolaevamariya/Dreamstime; p. 4 right bottom Richard
Thomas/Dreamstime; p. 5 first row right Ghassan Safi/Dreamstime; p. 5 second row left Lyudmila Suvorova/
Shutterstock; p. 5 second row middle Krischam/Dreamstime; p. 5 third row left Juan Moyano/Dreamstime;
p. 5 third row middle Swissmargrit/Dreamstime; p. 5 third row right (left to right) Crackerclips/Dreamstime;
Les Cunliffe/Dreamstime; Jerryb8/Dreamstime; p. 5 fourth row left AnutkaT/Shutterstock; p. 5 fourth row
right (left to right clockwise) Arinahabich08/Dreamstime; antpkr/Thinkstock; Kelpfish/Dreamstime; Vasiliy
Koval/Dreamstime; Jirk4/Dreamstime; Gradts/Dreamstime; sodapix sodapix/Thinkstock; p. 6 top Jakub
Krechowicz/Dreamstime; p. 6 middle Steveheap/Dreamstime; p. 9 top right Kmiragaya/Dreamstime; p. 10
top right Mimagephotography/Dreamstime; p. 11 top left Ryan Simpson/Dreamstime; p. 11 top right Dave
Bredeson/Dreamstime; p. 13 top right Gavril Margittai/Dreamstime; p. 15 top right Vlad Ivantcov/Dreamstime;
p. 17 top right Ppy2010ha/Dreamstime; p. 19 top right Elena Elisseeva/Dreamstime; p. 19 middle right Robert
Carner/Dreamstime; p. 21 top right Varandah/Dreamstime; p. 23 top right Ginasanders/Dreamstime; p. 25
top right Andres Rodriguez/Dreamstime; p. 27 top right Shawn And Sue Roberts/Dreamstime; p. 29 top right
David Dewhirst/Dreamstime.

Cataloging-in-Publication-Data
Reid, Emily.
I can make holiday gifts / by Emily Reid.
p. cm. — (Makerspace projects)
Includes index.
ISBN 978-1-4777-5639-3 (pbk.)
ISBN 978-1-4777-5638-6 (6 pack)
ISBN 978-1-4777-5562-4 (library binding)
1. Gifts — Juvenile literature.
2. Handicraft — Juvenile literature. I. Title.
TT160.R45 2016
745.5—d23

Manufactured in the United States of America
CPSIA Compliance Information: Batch #WS15WM: For Further Information contact: Rosen Publishing, New York, New York at 1-800-237-9932

CONTENTS

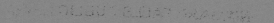

MATERIALS

To make great gifts, you need the right materials and a makerspace where you can think and create. Your family may have a permanent makerspace set up for crafting, or you can create one whenever you need it. You may already have many of the supplies shown here. Your family can buy anything else you need at a craft store or dollar store. Organize your supplies in boxes or plastic bins, and you will be ready to create in your makerspace.

A note about patterns

Many of the crafts in this book use patterns or **templates**. Trace the pattern, cut the pattern, and then place it on the material you want to cut out. You can either tape it in place and cut both the pattern and material, or trace around the pattern onto the material, and then cut it out.

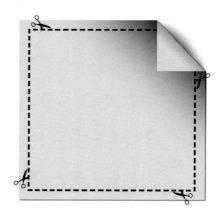

RECYCLABLES

You can make many of the crafts in this book with materials found around the house. Save recyclables (newspapers, cardboard boxes, mailing tubes, cereal boxes, tin cans, and more) to use in your craft projects.
Use your imagination and have fun!

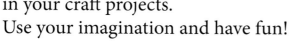

A note about measurements

Measurements are given in U.S. form with metric in brackets. The metric conversion is rounded to make it easier to measure.

PAINT AND MARKERS

TISSUE PAPER

GRAVEL

MAGNETS

MODELING CLAY

FABRIC

GLUE AND TAPE

PAPER

TOOLS

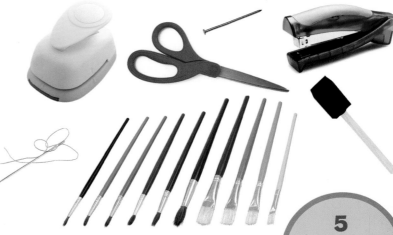

5

TECHNIQUES

Have fun while making your gifts! Be creative. Your project does not have to look just like the one in this book. If you don't have a certain material, think of something similar you could use.

The following techniques will help you create your crafts.

Using your creativity to make crafts is a very rewarding activity. When you are finished, you can say with great pride, **"I made that!"**

THREADING A NEEDLE

Threading a needle can be frustrating. The following tips will help.

- Cut more thread than you think you will need.
- Wet one end of the thread in your mouth.
- Poke it through the needle opening.
- Pull some of the thread through until you have an even amount and make a double knot.
- If you are using thicker thread like embroidery thread, do not double up the thread. Just pull a small amount through and make the knot at the other end.

EASIEST METHOD

- Use a metal needle threader.
- Push the metal threader through the needle hole, put the thread through the loop, and then pull the needle threader back through the needle.

Once the thread is in the loop, pull the loop back through the needle.

Put the thread through the loop.

SEWING FABRIC

The whipstitch works great with felt. It is used to sew two pieces together.
- Place the needle and knotted thread in between the two pieces of felt and up through the top layer of felt.
- Take the needle behind both layers of felt at point 1.
- Pull the needle through both layers of felt at point 2.
- Continue stitching until finished.

PAPER-MACHE CLAY RECIPE (REQUIRES THE USE OF A BLENDER)

- 2 cups (480 ml) newspaper torn into little pieces
- 4 cups (960 ml) water
- 1/2 cup (120 ml) water mixed with 1/2 cup (120 ml) flour

Mix in a blender 4 cups of water and 2 cups of newspaper pieces. (It is a good idea to do this in two stages.) After blending the newspaper pour the mixture into a fine mesh colander and squeeze the water out. Transfer to a bowl used for craft projects. Add the water and flour mixture and knead it together with your hands. It should have the consistency of clay.

SADDLE STITCH

Sew from outside to inside through hole 5.

Sew from inside to outside through hole 4.

Sew back through holes 2 and 3.

Sew from inside to outside through hole 1.

Sew from outside to inside through hole 2.

⑤ ④ ③ ② ①

Sew back through holes 4 and 5 and back to 3.

Start sewing from inside to outside through hole 3 leaving a length of string on the inside.

Make a small knot on the outside of hole 3. Make a small knot on the inside of hole 3.

BE PREPARED

- Read through the instructions and make sure you have all the materials you need.
- Cover your work area with newspaper or cardboard.
- Clean up your makerspace when you are finished making your project.

BE SAFE

- Ask for help when you need it.
- Ask for permission to borrow tools.
- Be careful when using knives, scissors, and sewing needles.

VASE

Make a beautiful vase with a glass bottle or jar and tissue paper. Give your gift with a bunch of flowers.

You'll Need

- ✔ Colored tissue paper
- ✔ Scissors
- ✔ Glue (dries clear)
- ✔ Small container
- ✔ Popsicle stick
- ✔ Brush
- ✔ Glass jar (labels removed)
- ✔ Shape punch (optional)
- ✔ Ribbon (optional)

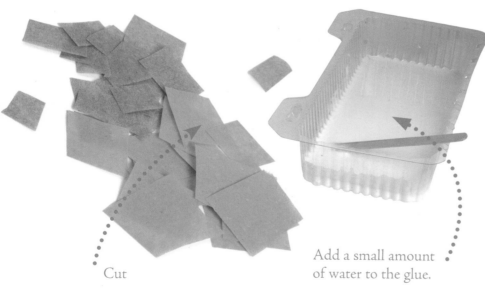

Stick tissue paper to the glue.

Cut

Add a small amount of water to the glue.

1 Tear or cut several different colors of tissue paper into small pieces.

2 Pour glue into a container. Add a small amount of water. Stir with a popsicle stick.

3 Brush glue onto the jar. Apply pieces of tissue paper to the glue.

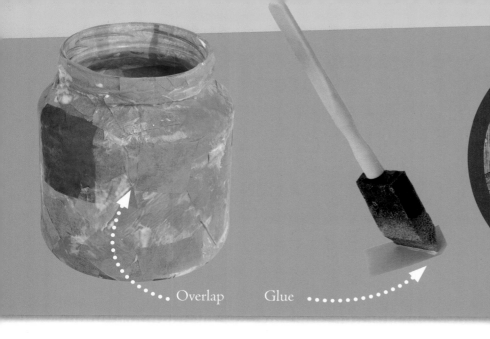

Overlap   Glue

Did You Know?

People have been making vases for at least 3,000 years. Vases are found at historic sites all over the world.

4 Start overlapping the squares. Add glue to the tissue paper and stick to the jar. Continue until the jar is completely covered.

Add ribbon.

Add shapes.

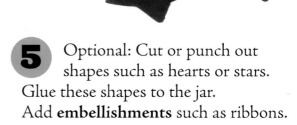

5 Optional: Cut or punch out shapes such as hearts or stars. Glue these shapes to the jar. Add **embellishments** such as ribbons.

6 Brush the remaining glue over the vase. Leave to dry.

Tip
To cut out many squares of tissue paper, fold a big piece over and over until you are left with a small square. Cut each edge off and you have many squares!

Another Idea!

Do this craft with regular paper too. Save used wrapping paper and recycle it into vases.

MOSAIC FRAME

Give a photo of yourself or a photo you took framed in a mosaic frame you created.

You'll Need

- ✔ Wood or cardboard frame
- ✔ Paint and brush
- ✔ Gravel in various colors (found in the aquarium section of a department store or pet store)
- ✔ Glue and stick or brush
- ✔ Googly eyes, small rocks, or stick-on gems (optional)
- ✔ Small container

Sort the gravel.

Paint the frame.

Glue the gravel.

1 Paint the wood or cardboard frame with paint. Paint the sides of the frame too.

2 Prepare a work area. Lay some paper out. Plan the design. Separate each color of gravel that you plan to use.

3 Apply glue to a section of the frame. Spread it around with a brush or stick. Apply the gravel to the glue-covered areas according to your design.

Add glass rocks.

4 Continue adding glue and more gravel until the entire frame is covered. Optional: when applying the gravel to the glue, add other decorations such as googly eyes, small rocks, or stick-on gems.

5 In a container, mix equal parts of water and glue and brush this mixture over all the gravel. Don't brush it over the rocks or googly eyes.

Cover the frame with varnish made from glue and water.

Did You Know?

Picture frames date back to ancient Egypt. In the Middle Ages, frames for religious art were carved by hand and decorated with gold and jewels.

Tip

Make sure all the gravel has been glued on well. After leaving it to dry turn the frame over and if any pieces fall off glue them back on.

Another Idea!

Use different colors of card stock for the mosaic. Cut the card stock into small pieces with scissors. Glue the pieces to the frame. Varnish the frame with watered-down glue.

T-SHIRT PILLOW

Make a pillow out of a T-shirt to give as a gift.

You'll Need

✔ Quilt batting or fiberfill
✔ Tapestry needle
✔ Thread
✔ T-shirt
✔ Scissors
✔ String
✔ Ribbon
✔ Paint and brush (optional)

Roll the quilt batting and stitch in place.

Sew

Turn the fabric right side out.

1 Roll the quilt batting to make a pillow form. Thread the needle and sew the end of the roll in place.

2 Cut a 14-inch (36 cm) square from the T-shirt with one end being the sides. Fold in half. Sew the top edges together using the whipstitch (directions on page 6).

3 Turn the fabric so the right side is out (still doubled).

Place the quilt batting in the T-shirt tube.

Did You Know?

Feathers, rags, or straw were used to fill pillows before **synthetic** materials such as polyester became available.

4 Pull the pillow form into the T-shirt tube. Center the stuffing in the middle of the tube. Push the stuffing in until you have about 2½ inches (6½ cm) of T-shirt at either end.

Tie a bow with ribbon.

Wrap and tie string.

5 Cut two pieces of string. Wrap one piece of string tightly around one end and tie it. Wrap the string around five more times and tie in a knot. Repeat for the other end. Trim the string.

6 Squish the pillow until the shape is pleasing. Fluff the T-shirt ends to resemble a rosette. Cut two pieces of ribbon. Tie a ribbon around each end and make a bow. Optional: paint some flowers or other design on the pillow.

Another Idea!

Make a square T-shirt pillow. Cut a T-shirt just below the sleeves. Turn inside out. Sew the top end together and most of the bottom as in step 2. Turn the pillow right side out. Place the quilt batting in the pillow. Sew the last opening closed.

FRIDGE MAGNETS

Make a cute set of magnets to give as a gift. Use air-drying clay and cookie cutters to make them.

You'll Need

- ✔ Air-drying clay
- ✔ Rolling pin
- ✔ Wax paper (or parchment paper)
- ✔ Mini cookie cutters or butter knife
- ✔ Paint
- ✔ Brush
- ✔ Glue
- ✔ Small magnets

Roll out.   Cut out.   Add shapes..

1 Using air-drying clay and an old rolling pin, roll your clay into a ¼-inch (1 cm) slab. Make sure you put something like wax paper under and over the clay as it may stain your countertop. Start in the middle and roll away and then roll towards yourself.

2 Use cookie cutters or a butter knife to cut your shapes. Press them into the clay and then gently push the clay out of the cookie cutter. You can flatten the shape further or bend it. Make an indentation if you want to add a gemstone later.

3 You can add texture, such as clay dots for eyes, by a process called **score and slip**. Make a shallow groove with a butter knife where you want to add a shape, and add a bit of water. This acts like clay glue. Attach your shape to the spot.

Leave them to dry.

4 Let the shapes dry overnight on a flat surface.

5 When your shapes are dry, you can paint them. Painting them white first will make the colors on top even brighter.

Paint

6 If you want them to be shiny, mix a little white glue and water. Use this mixture to cover your painted shapes.

Cover with glue and water mixture for a shiny surface.

7 Once everything is dry, glue the magnet onto the back of the shape.

Add glue.

Attach magnet.

Tip

A fun idea would be to make letters that spell someone's name. Make a magnet for each one of the letters in their name!

FABRIC BOWLS

Bowls are a great gift to give. They are great for storing many different items.

You'll Need

- ✔ Tray covered in wax paper or cardboard to work on
- ✔ Bowl
- ✔ Plastic wrap
- ✔ Fabric
- ✔ Scissors
- ✔ Glue (that dries clear)
- ✔ Foam brush

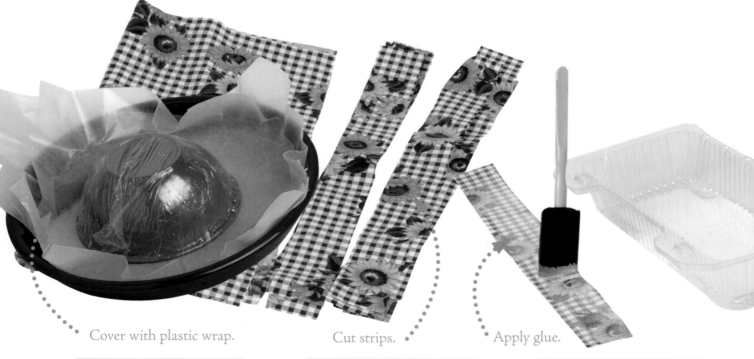

Cover with plastic wrap.

Cut strips.

Apply glue.

1 Cover the outside of the bowl with plastic wrap. Place the bowl bottom side up on the tray or cardboard.

2 Cut fabric strips about 1 inch (2.5 cm) wide and long enough to go over the bowl.

3 Pour glue into a container. Brush glue on the right side (print side if there is a pattern) of a fabric strip.

Lay strip glue side
down on the bowl.

4 Lay the fabric strip on the bowl, glue side down.
Smooth it out. Lay another strip over the bowl.
Continue until the bowl is covered.

Did You Know?

Early peoples used
shells, gourds, and
leaves for bowls. Over
time people learned to
make bowls of wood,
leather, metal, pottery,
glass, and plastic.

Spread glue over
the whole bowl.

Cover the bowl with strips
right side facing up.

Trim the edges.

5 Brush glue over the
covered bowl until
it is covered in a thin layer.

6 Brush glue over the wrong
side of a strip and lay it
over the bowl as in step 4.
Continue until the bowl is
covered. This time the right
side of the fabric is showing.

7 Brush a layer of
glue over the whole
bowl again. Leave to dry.
Remove the bowl. Trim
the edges of the fabric bowl
with scissors.

Another Idea!

Use a print fabric for the
outside of the bowl and
solid color fabric for the
inside. Experiment with
different-sized bowls.

BIRD FEEDER

Many people like to feed wild birds. There is nothing more delightful than watching wild birds roam your garden.

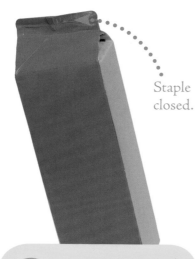

You'll Need

- ✔ Milk carton (clean and dry)
- ✔ Stapler
- ✔ Paint and brush
- ✔ Ruler
- ✔ Pen
- ✔ Nail
- ✔ Scissors
- ✔ Clear packing tape
- ✔ Twine
- ✔ Twig or **dowel**

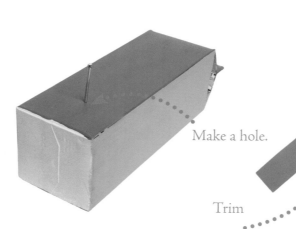

Staple closed.

Make a hole.

Trim

1 Staple carton top shut. Paint the carton, or cover it with paper and tape the paper in place.

2 Measure 1½ inches (4 cm) up from the bottom on the front, make a mark. Repeat on the back. Use a nail to make two holes for the twig or dowel.

3 Draw a line ½ inch (1.3 cm) above the hole. Measure 3½ inches (9 cm) above the line and make another line. Cut across the bottom line and at the sides up to the top line. Press the flap out and cut about 2 inches (5 cm) off. Repeat on the other side.

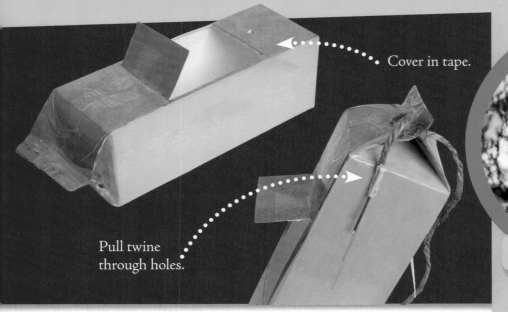

Cover in tape.

Pull twine through holes.

4 Cut pieces of packing tape and cover the carton. Overlap the tape and continue until the carton is covered. Use a nail to make two holes through the top of the carton. Tape the twine to the nail and pull it through the two holes.

Did You Know?

Black oil sunflower seeds are a favorite of many wild birds, including colorful blue jays and cardinals.

5 Remove the nail and knot the ends.

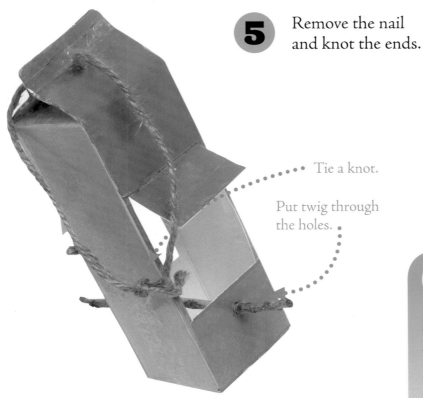

Tie a knot.

Put twig through the holes.

Another Idea!

An aluminum pie plate holds the birdseed for this super-simple bird feeder. Poke four holes in the plate with a nail and tie a piece of twine at each hole. Tie the four ends of twine together leaving extra twine. Make another knot and you have a loop to hang it from a tree.

6 Push the nail through the tape covering the holes made for the twig or dowel. Place the twig or dowel through the holes.

NOTE CARDS

Note cards are a wonderful way to send a thank-you to someone. Give a set of note cards to someone special.

You'll Need

- Potato
- Star cookie cutter
- Plastic knife
- Shallow container
- Acrylic paint
- Brush
- Card stock in white and colors
- Scissors
- String or ribbon
- Glue or tape
- Double-sided tape

Press the cookie cutter into the potato.

Press the potato onto the card stock.

1 Cut a potato in half. Press the cookie cutter into the potato. Carve the excess away from the shape with a plastic knife.

2 Using a paintbrush, spread a thin coat of paint into the container. Press the star end of the potato into the paint. You can also use the brush to paint onto the potato directly.

3 Press the paint-coated potato onto the white card stock. Experiment with printing without adding more paint.

Fold color card stock in half.

Cut white card stock.

Did You Know?

Potato printing uses a process called relief printing. Many historians believe it was first used in ancient China, where images were carved onto wooden blocks for stamping. Paper for stamping on was invented in China, too!

4 Make cards. Fold the colored card stock in half. Cut the white card stock with the design into a smaller piece.

Make a stamp with bubble wrap.

Make a stamp with a sponge.

Apply double-sided tape.

5 Wrap a ribbon or string around the card stock and tape or glue it on the back. Place two strips of double-sided tape or glue on the back of the white card stock. Press it to the front of the card.

Tip
To get an even fold, line the corners up and press towards the middle. Run the edge of a ruler over the fold after to make it crisp.

Another Idea!

Make other stamps. Squeeze the middle of a square sponge to look like a bow. Press it into paint and then onto card stock. Rock it as you press to get corners. Glue a piece of bubble wrap to a sponge and dip in paint and then onto card stock. Try stamping with the cookie cutter itself.

PAPER COASTERS

You can give a useful and unusual looking set of coasters as a gift. The receiver will appreciate the time and effort.

You'll Need

✔ Newspapers
✔ Scissors
✔ Long wood skewers
✔ White glue (that dries clear)
✔ Brush
✔ Felt

Cut in strips.

Start rolling from a corner.

1 Cut strips of newspaper 4 inches (10 cm) wide by 11 inches (28 cm) long. Choose pages with some color so that the finished piece has some color in it.

2 Using a long wood skewer, roll the newspaper strips into long thin tubes. Use white glue to secure the end of the tube. Slide the tube from the skewer.

3 Flatten each tube with your finger or the edge of a ruler.

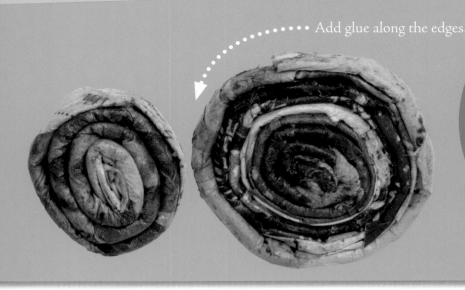

Add glue along the edges.

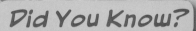

Did You Know?

Many products are made from recycled newspaper. They include cereal boxes, egg cartons, grocery bags, tissue paper, insulation, animal bedding, and more newspaper.

4 Apply glue to the edge of the thin tube. Start rolling it in a circle. Keep adding more tubes and more glue around the circle until you reach the desired size.

Cut a piece of felt.

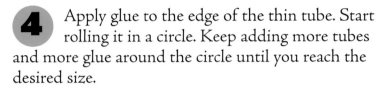

5 Use a brush to cover the top of the coil with a mixture of glue and water (equal parts). Leave it to dry.

Glue the felt to the coil.

6 Cut a piece of felt that is the same size as the coil. Apply glue to the felt. Place the felt on top of the coil. Leave to dry. Make another one!

Tip

If the coil is not staying glued while you roll the tube, put a rubber band around the coil and let it dry a few minutes before continuing.

Another Idea!

Make original wall art using several large circles done with this technique.

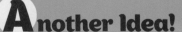

DESK SET

Give the gift of a desk set. It is great for keeping pens, pencils, and paper clips organized.

You'll Need

- Plain and patterned paper
- Scissors
- Tin cans (3)
- Double-sided tape
- Glue
- Yarn or string
- Felt
- Marker

Add glue to the paper.

1 Cut a piece of plain paper slightly longer than the tin can and wide enough to wrap around and overlap slightly. Attach double-sided tape to the tin can at the top and bottom.

2 Fold the bottom of the paper over and tape it to the bottom of the can.

3 Glue the top end of the yarn or string on the can. Leave a piece to hang down the can and cover it with more yarn as the yarn goes around the can. Add glue to the paper as the yarn is wound around. Cut the yarn when you reach the bottom.

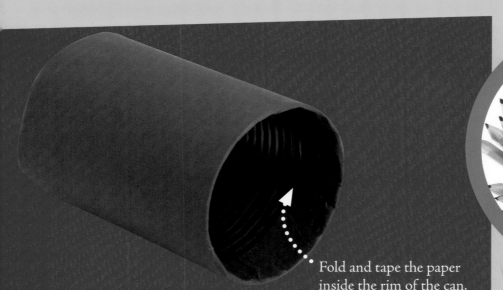

Fold and tape the paper inside the rim of the can.

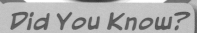
4 Cover the other two cans with yarn or with patterned paper as in steps 1 and 2. Optional: cut the paper longer and fold and tape some paper over the rim and inside the can.

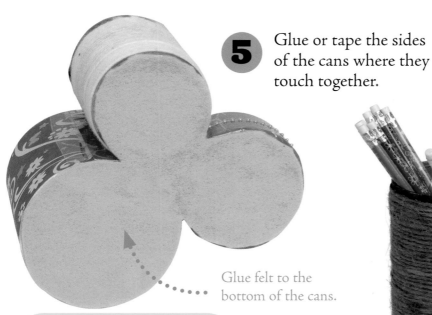

5 Glue or tape the sides of the cans where they touch together.

Glue felt to the bottom of the cans.

6 Place the cans on a piece of felt. Trace around the bottom of the cans with a marker. Cut the felt out and glue to the bottom of the cans.

Tip
Glue or tape the three seams of the cans together so that none of the paper seams face out.

Another Idea!
Add embellishments such as charms to one of the cans using twine or string. You also could glue beads or gems to the cans.

25

JOURNAL

A handmade journal is a gift that will be treasured. It can be **customized** by the selection of cover paper.

You'll Need

- ✔ Letter-sized paper (16 sheets)
- ✔ Pencil
- ✔ Scissors
- ✔ Poster board
- ✔ Glue
- ✔ Nail
- ✔ Hammer
- ✔ String or lightweight twine (2 feet or 61 cm)
- ✔ Tapestry needle
- ✔ Craft paper
- ✔ Ribbon

Fold

Hammer nails through.

1 Fold the 16 pages of paper in half. Stack them one inside the other. Open to the middle of the stack. With a pencil, make five evenly spaced marks along the fold.

2 Cut 9 x 11-inch (23 x 28 cm) pieces of poster board and craft paper for the cover. Glue the craft paper to the poster board. Cut a smaller piece of craft paper and glue down the center. Fold in half. Make five evenly spaced marks in the same places as the paper.

3 Place a magazine or something similar under the paper. With a nail and hammer make holes at the indicated spots on the paper and cover.

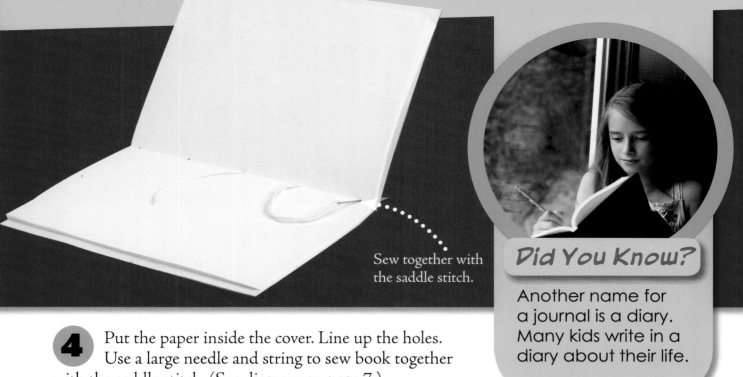

Sew together with the saddle stitch.

4 Put the paper inside the cover. Line up the holes. Use a large needle and string to sew book together with the saddle stitch. (See diagram on page 7.)

5 Cut two strips of craft paper 2½ inches (6 cm) wide and the same length as the cover. Cut two equal lengths of ribbon.

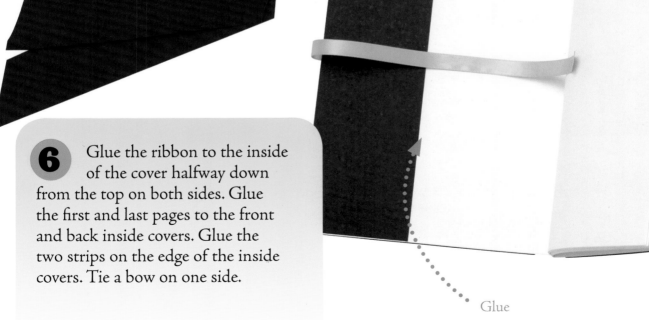

6 Glue the ribbon to the inside of the cover halfway down from the top on both sides. Glue the first and last pages to the front and back inside covers. Glue the two strips on the edge of the inside covers. Tie a bow on one side.

Glue

PAPER-MACHE OWL

Give someone a cheerful-looking paper-mache bird to brighten their home or office.

You'll Need

- ✔ Paper for tracing
- ✔ Thin cardboard
- ✔ Tape
- ✔ Scissors
- ✔ Newspaper
- ✔ Paper towel
- ✔ Instant paper-mache (or mash from recipe on page 7)
- ✔ Plastic bag
- ✔ Paint
- ✔ Paintbrush
- ✔ Glue

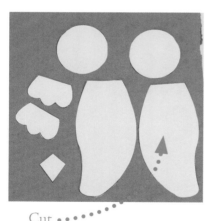

Cut

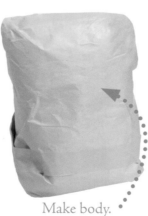

Make body.

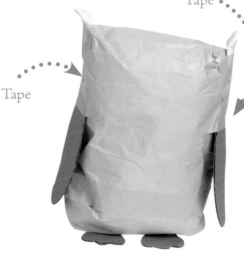

Tape

Tape

1 Trace the pattern pieces on page 31 onto paper. Tape the pattern pieces to thin cardboard. Use scissors to cut the cardboard pieces out.

2 Form the body by squishing newspaper into an oval shape about 6½ inches (16.5 cm) tall by 5½ inches (14 cm) wide and about 4½ inches (11 cm) deep.

3 Tape a piece of paper towel to the top of the head to form ears. Tape the wings to the side of the body. Tape the feet to the bottom.

Mix the paper-mache paste.

4 Prepare a work area with newspaper. Mix your instant paper-mache according to the directions on the box or the recipe on page 7. Mix it directly in a plastic bag for easier storage of the leftovers. The mixture above is good for molding directly. Add more water for a thinner paste for putting on the form.

Cover the entire form with the paper-mache mixture.

5 Start adding the paper-mache mixture all over the form. Smooth it out. Cover the eyes and beak shapes and stick to the head. Keep adding more until the whole form is covered. Leave it to dry.

Paint

6 Paint the owl in cheerful colors. Leave to dry. Mix a little white glue and water. Use this mixture to cover your owl with a protective varnish.

Tip
You can reuse the paper-mache, just wrap it tightly in a plastic bag. It will keep for several weeks in the fridge.

Another Idea!
Mold some of the paper-mache into a bird shape without using a form. Leave to dry overnight. Paint.

WRAPPING YOUR GIFTS

A wonderful gift is even better when it is beautifully wrapped. Create a gift box with wrapping that can even be re-used!

You'll Need

- ✔ Boxes with lids
- ✔ Wrapping paper
- ✔ Scissors
- ✔ Glue
- ✔ Double-sided tape
- ✔ Ribbon
- ✔ Stapler

Tape

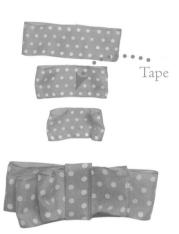

Tape

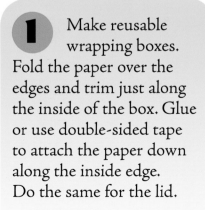

Tape

1 Make reusable wrapping boxes. Fold the paper over the edges and trim just along the inside of the box. Glue or use double-sided tape to attach the paper down along the inside edge. Do the same for the lid.

2 Cut strips of ribbon just longer than the box. Use glue or double-sided tape to attach them to the box, folding the end just over the edge of the box. Glue or use double-sided tape to attach matching ribbon to the lid. Glue or tape a bow in the center of the lid.

3 Make a bow. Cut three pieces of ribbon, 4 inches (10 cm), 3½ inches (9 cm) and 3 inches (7.5 cm) long. Tape each end together. Layer them so the smallest is on top and staple. Cut another piece of ribbon. Fold it in half and wrap it around the center and tape it on the bottom.

PATTERNS

Pattern for the owl on page 28.

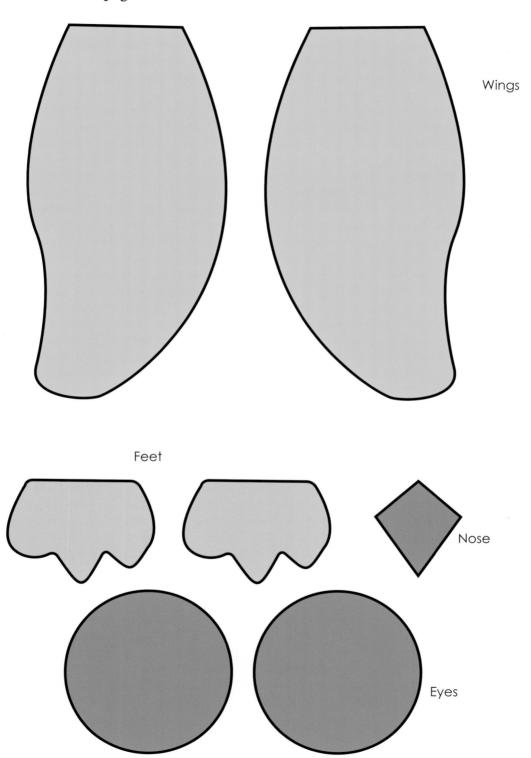

Wings

Feet

Nose

Eyes

GLOSSARY

customized Made or changed to suit a certain person or purpose.

dowel A peg or stick used to hold pieces together.

embellishments Decorations.

score and slip Make a shallow groove (score) and add water (slip); used to join clay pieces.

synthetic Artificial; not from nature.

template A shape used as a pattern.

FOR MORE INFORMATION

FURTHER READING

DK Publishing. *Make Your Own Gifts.*
New York, NY: DK Publishing, 2013.

Hantman, Clea. *I Wanna Make Gifts.*
New York, NY: Simon and Schuster, 2010.

Nichols, Kaitlyn. *Make Clay Charms.*
Palo Alto, CA: Klutz, 2013.

WEBSITES

For web resources related to the subject of this book, go to:
www.windmillbooks.com/weblinks and select this book's title.

INDEX